HELLO KITTY and friends

The Beach Holiday

The Beach Holiday

HarperCollins *Children's Books*

MEET
HELLO KITTY
and friends
Mimmy
Hello Kitty
Tammy

Mama
Papa
Grandpa
Grandma
Dear Daniel
Fifi

With special thanks to
Linda Chapman and Michelle Misra

First published in Great Britain by HarperCollins *Children's Books* in 2013

www.harpercollins.co.uk
1 3 5 7 9 10 8 6 4 2
ISBN: 978-000-751443-4

Printed and bound in England by Clays Ltd, St Ives plc.

Contents

1

Holiday Plans

Hello Kitty skipped around the kitchen table putting out her favourite pink stripy plates. She was excited because her friends Tammy and Fifi were coming over to her house for a Friendship Club meeting! The three girls and Dear Daniel had started the Friendship Club a little while ago. They held meetings, went on trips out and made up rules about being a good friend. It was really great fun!

Hello Kitty folded some pink serviettes into triangles and put one neatly on each plate. She couldn't **wait** until the meeting – they had so much to talk about! A little while ago,

Tammy's parents had invited them all to go away for three nights to a little holiday cottage which was next to a sandy beach. It would be the very first Friendship Club holiday – how *exciting* was that? Unfortunately, Dear Daniel couldn't go because he was travelling with his dad, but he had told them to have a great time and made them promise to tell him all about it when he got back. They were setting off to the cottage the very next day.

Hello Kitty arranged

some freshly-baked chocolate chip cookies on to a plate. She had just made them! She fetched some lemonade and found pink straws for the cups.

Just then there was a **knock** at the front door. Hello Kitty raced to open it and found that Mama had beaten her to it – Fifi and Tammy were standing on the doorstep! The girls hugged and said hello and then all ran into the kitchen together.

Soon the three friends were sitting around the table, munching happily. The cookies were still warm and the chocolate slightly melted. **Yum!** Everyone wanted to talk about the

holiday – what they would do, where they would go, what they would pack. Hello Kitty opened her sparkly notepad and suggested that they make a list of all the things they might like to do while they were away. The others started to call things out...

- Make sandcastles
- Eat ice cream
- Go swimming in the sea
- Go on a boat trip

Hello Kitty added some ideas of her own...

- Collect shells
- Go to a fun fair
- Explore rock pools
- Dance on the sand

They all grinned at each other when she stopped writing. This was going to be the best holiday ever! Tammy warned Hello Kitty and Fifi that her twin brother Timmy would be there too, and that they might have to watch out – he loved playing tricks! He went to their school but was in a different class – he had the same teacher as Hello Kitty's twin sister, Mimmy. But Hello Kitty had an idea. **Maybe** Timmy would like to join the Friendship Club?

Tammy shook her head. She had asked him if he wanted to join when they had first started it but Timmy had told her he didn't have time because he was always out playing football.

Hello Kitty understood. Everyone had different things they liked doing and they would still all be able to enjoy the holiday together! She turned the page in her notebook. It was time to make a list of all the things they should bring...

Books.

Swimsuits

Buckets and spades.

Sunscreen.

Shorts and

T-shirts

Suddenly Hello Kitty had a great idea! For the rest of the Friendship Club meeting why didn't they each choose their **perfect** beach outfit from the clothes they had at home? The others thought that sounded fun and so they all set

to work, drawing and colouring. By going-home time the three friends had each drawn several outfits. Now they just had to get ready to pack them into their suitcases!

Hello Kitty waved goodbye and then shut the door, excitement *fizzing* inside her. She could hardly wait for the morning to come!

Setting Off!

Hello Kitty jumped out of bed the next morning and ran to open her curtains. The sky was clear and blue and the sun was shining down. What a completely super day for going on holiday!

Hello Kitty had put her clothes out neatly the night before. She had decided to wear bright pink shorts, a white T-shirt with a big pink heart on, and polka dot socks with sneakers.

She got dressed, brushed her hair and then clipped on a polka dot bow. She finished her look with a little dash of Raspberry Ripple lip balm. **There!** She twirled round. She was all ready to go!

Just then, her twin sister Mimmy came into

Hello Kitty's room. She was **also** getting ready to go away. She and her friend Alice were going to flute camp for a few days. Mimmy thought it would be very strange being without each other but then Hello Kitty reminded her what **fun** they would have talking about their holidays when they finally got home! The two sisters gave each other a hug and then hurried downstairs to have breakfast.

Mama White had made pancakes. **Yummy!** Hello Kitty poured chocolate sauce on hers and Mimmy had maple syrup. They ate everything up, brushed their teeth and then it was time for Hello Kitty to go.

Papa had taken the day off work so he could say goodbye to Hello Kitty and Mimmy. Tammy's parents drove up in their big silver car, and Tammy, Timmy and Fifi waved from the window as Hello Kitty *raced* out to greet them. Papa put her suitcase in the boot and then Hello Kitty kissed her family goodbye and climbed into the back with all her friends. This was so exciting! The back of the car was piled high with suitcases, beach balls, tennis racquets and fishing nets. There was hardly any room to squeeze in!

Hello Kitty waved as Tammy's dad drove them off.

As they headed towards the cottage, Hello Kitty thought of all the other

exciting things that the Friendship Club had done. She reminded Fifi and Tammy of the summer fair they had organised for the animal shelter and the time they had all gone to a concert and danced on stage. Tammy remembered when they

had gone climbing through trees at Monkey Madness and when they had watched Fifi in an ice-skating competition.

Tammy's mum laughed. The Friendship Club always had a lot of **fun**. They had done so many things! Timmy agreed. Hello Kitty thought he looked a bit left out, so she asked him if he would like to join the Friendship Club after all.

Timmy was really pleased. He said he wouldn't have time when they were back at school because of football practice but he would **love** to join the Friendship Club for the holiday.

The girls grinned. Now they were all members! How super was that?

Tammy's mum asked if they had thought of what they would like to do on holiday, so Hello Kitty read out the list they had made.

There was a laugh from Tammy's dad. He told them they would be able to do **lots** of those things, although they probably wouldn't have time to go to a fun fair *and* go on a boat trip as well. Hello Kitty hoped they could at least go out on a boat, since they were staying beside the sea, but she tried not to think about it. After all, it was much better to think of all the things you could do than the things you couldn't!

They played I-Spy and ate some barley sugar and then Tammy's mum suggested they sing some songs to make the journey go quicker. That sounded fun! Soon they were all singing *One Hundred Green Bottles* as the car headed onwards towards the sea. They were going to be there in no time at all!

The holiday cottage was down a little lane beside the sea. It was painted white and had wooden tubs filled with **bright** flowers on either side of its blue front door. There was a little walled garden with emerald-green grass and beyond the garden was a path leading over a small cliff to the sandy beach and the sea.

As Hello Kitty got out of the car she took a deep breath of the salty air. What a beautiful place! The sea sparkled in the sunlight and there were little white crests on the waves. She hoped they could go and play on the beach soon but first there was the unpacking to do.

Tammy's mum unlocked the cottage and the girls and Timmy took their suitcases and bags inside. Downstairs there was a kitchen with a big table and a cosy lounge with big French windows that opened on to the garden. Upstairs there were three bedrooms – one for Tammy's parents, one for Timmy and one for the girls. They all hurried into their bedrooms to unpack. The one for the three girls was **lovely!** It had bright sunshine yellow walls and big windows. There were three beds, a big white dressing table with a round mirror, and two chests of drawers. The girls split the drawers between them, took all the clothes out of their suitcases and put them away. Tammy and Hello Kitty folded their clothes neatly but Fifi just **stuffed** everything into her drawers. She wasn't quite so good at being neat and tidy!

Whilst Hello Kitty arranged her lip balms and Tammy sorted her books into a neat pile, Fifi did handstands against the wall. She wanted to run outside and play, not spend her time unpacking!

Soon Hello Kitty and Tammy were ready to go. They all turned to head out of the room when suddenly…

BOO!

They all squealed and almost fell over as Timmy jumped out at them from

behind a chair on the landing.

He laughed and laughed.

Tammy shook her head. Sometimes her brother was really annoying! They must have looked quite funny, though, jumping like that, Hello Kitty pointed out, and Tammy smiled. Laughing all together with Timmy, they hurried downstairs.

Tammy's mum was unpacking the kitchen things. They offered to help her but she suggested they run along and explore the beach instead. It was a little too chilly to swim but they could still explore and play on the sand! Tammy's dad would go with them and she would bring a picnic lunch out for everyone in a little while.

They all helped Tammy's dad get the things they needed for the beach from the car.

They took along their buckets and spades, beach towels, and a beach ball.

Finally they were all ready to go! Hello Kitty gave a little skip of delight. Their holiday was about to begin!

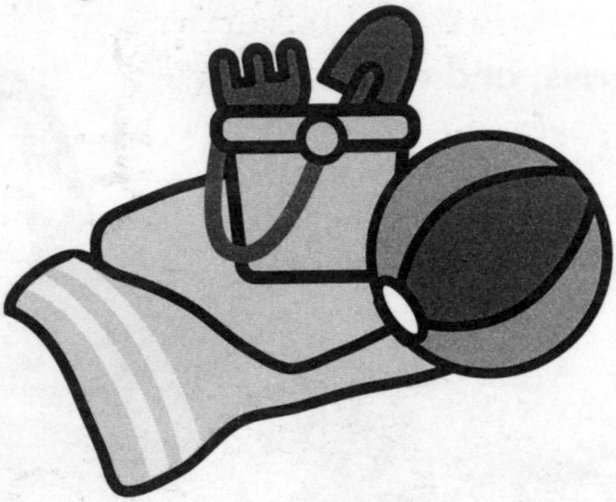

3

Too Many Tricks

A little path led over the small cliff and down to the beach. Hello Kitty and her friends skipped along it until they came out on the golden sand. The tide had gone out and had left glittering rock pools and piles of shells on the wet sand, but the sand by the cliffs was soft and dry. Tammy's dad set up his deckchair there.

Timmy wanted to run out to the sea and paddle in it but Fifi was worried there might be jellyfish in the sea. She didn't like jellyfish

at all!

So Hello Kitty suggested that they collect shells and make a sandcastle instead.

Timmy ran off to the water while the girls set to work with the buckets and spades. They built

an **amazing** sandcastle that looked like a fairytale palace with turrets and a moat. While Fifi and Tammy fetched shells and seaweed to decorate it, Hello Kitty went to one of the rock pools to scoop up some water to fill the moat. She was just bending over with her bucket when there was a loud yell, and Timmy jumped out from behind a rock and **leaped** into the middle of the pool! Water splashed everywhere, soaking Hello Kitty from top to toe! She called out in surprise. Timmy grinned.

What a good trick he'd played!

Hello Kitty wasn't sure about that. She was wet all over now. Still, she knew she would dry quickly. She picked up her bucket full of water and headed back to the sandcastle.

Timmy danced alongside her. As soon as he got to the sandcastle, he started pretending that he was about to jump on it.

After a little while Tammy got cross and told him to go away, so he ran off to the nearest rock pool. He put his hands in the water and pulled out something green. He cried out that it was a jellyfish and came running back towards the girls. Fifi was not happy at all! She

squealed unhappily and ran away, and Timmy chased her.

Tammy *raced* after him and grabbed his arm to tell him to stop – Fifi was really quite scared! She wasn't afraid of many things but she had once been stung by a jellyfish when she was little and she had been frightened of them ever since.

Timmy felt a bit sorry for scaring Fifi. It had just been a joke. He showed them that the jellyfish he was pretending to hold was just a clump of seaweed, and Fifi blushed bright pink.

Just then Tammy's dad came over. He had seen what had happened and thought that maybe Timmy should explore the cliff with him while the girls finished their castle in peace! The cliffs were too steep to climb but there were some fun small caves at the base of them. Maybe there would be some

treasure there...

So Timmy went off with his dad and the girls finished the Friendship Club castle. They

made it look beautiful by decorating it with pink round shells, some little bits of green glass polished smooth by the sea, and some green ribbon seaweed. And they put a little flag they made out of a shell and Hello Kitty's purple hanky on top!

By the time they had finished, it looked **perfect.** Hello Kitty wished she was small enough to live in it herself! Tammy imagined a little sea fairy finding it and making it her home.

She was very good at **dreaming** up stories. Fifi and Hello Kitty sat down on the sand while Tammy made up a story about the little sea fairy and a mean sea sprite who played tricks. In the end, the sea sprite was sorry about the tricks he played, and he and the fairy became best friends.

Tammy's story gave Hello Kitty an idea. They should all tell stories about mermaids and sea fairies that night when they went to bed!

The others thought that was a super idea.

As they were chatting about the stories they would tell, they heard Tammy's dad calling them. He and Timmy were waving from over where they had been exploring the cliffs. They hadn't found any treasure, but they had found Tammy's mum with her hands full of ice cream tubs!

The girls ran over and soon everyone was sitting on the soft sand eating yummy chocolate ice cream. What could be better than that?

4

Holiday Fun!

After they had played on the beach some more, they all had a picnic lunch and then headed back to the cottage. Fifi thought that maybe there would still be time for them to have a Friendship Club meeting. They could make Timmy a membership card and do some drawing. Hello Kitty put in that they could each design a bikini or swimsuit too, and Tammy suggested they make up a recipe for some special holiday fruit punch.

They got out the paper and pens and went to the small dining room where there was a table.

Timmy joined them but he didn't want to draw a swimsuit – he thought that sounded **boring**. And when Hello Kitty carefully made him a membership card with his photo on it, he got a felt tip pen and drew a moustache on to the picture. He really was so mischievous!

So Timmy decided to go and play in his room with his plastic monsters. Tammy sighed as he

left. She told the others she was sorry about the way her brother was acting. She wasn't sure why he was behaving in such a silly way. Hello Kitty and Fifi told her to forget about it – it was OK, really. They set to work finishing their swimsuit designs. Hello Kitty drew herself in a pink and blue **spotted** bikini with a matching sarong, Tammy drew herself in a rainbow-striped swimsuit and Fifi drew herself in a yellow tankini covered with pictures of palm trees with a matching parasol.

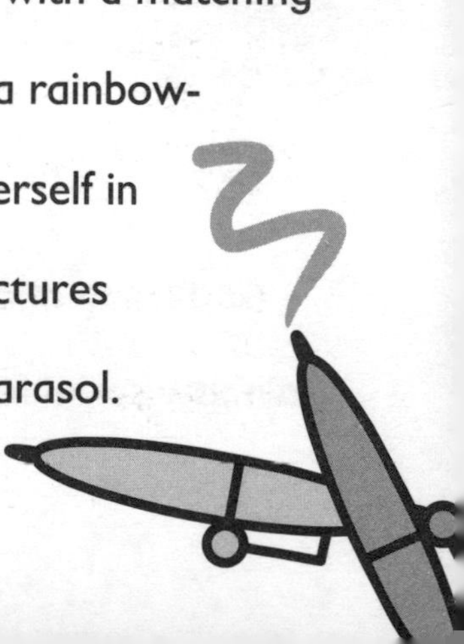

Afterwards, they started to make a list of ingredients for their special holiday Friendship Club punch. They decided they would mix together:

And a scoop of strawberry ice cream and rainbow sprinkles on top!

Luckily Tammy's mum had all the ingredients with her. They mixed them up and then added the scoop of ice cream and the sprinkles and stuck three straws in. It was the most **delicious** punch they had ever tasted!

Then it was time to help Tammy's mum get the food ready for the barbecue they were having for dinner. They made the salads for her, put out the bread rolls and carried the sausages out to Tammy's dad who was lighting the barbecue on the patio.

They were all a great help! Tammy's mum let them have a chocolate each while they were waiting for the barbecue to heat up.

Soon the **delicious** smell of sausages cooking wafted across the patio. Timmy came downstairs and helped his dad serve while Tammy's mum put on some music.

Finally, they sat down and ate while the sun set in the sky. It wasn't very late when they finished, but they were all ***SOOO*** tired from their long day that they decided to go upstairs to bed early. And then Hello Kitty remembered that Tammy was going to tell them stories about mermaids and sea fairies! Should they

invite Timmy, she asked? But Tammy said no. He would only laugh – he thought mermaids were silly, she whispered.

So the girls got into their pyjamas and **snuggled** under the duvet on Tammy's bed as she made up a story about an underwater kingdom and a mermaid princess who lived there.

It was a lovely story. The mermaid princess played with her friends and went out into the coral reef to have adventures. Hello Kitty and Fifi could see it all in their heads as Tammy described the world and what was happening. She was just telling them about how the mermaid princess found a cave in the reef one day and swam inside to see if she could find some hidden treasure when Timmy **threw** the bedroom door open and ran in waving a plastic shark!

Oh no! Not again! Timmy must have been listening outside the door. He said that rather than finding the treasure, the mermaid had found a shark and that it chased her and tried to eat her!

He ran at the girls, giggling and chasing them with the shark and making its jaws snap. They all jumped out of bed. Tammy yelled for Timmy to stop and then there was a knock at the door and their mum came in! She was not very happy that they were making so much **noise** when they were supposed to be settling down

for the night. She opened her mouth to say so, but Timmy was good and spoke very quickly before she could say anything at all. He stepped forward and told his mum that the noise was his fault and not the girls'. She held out her hand to him and took him off to his room.

Hello Kitty breathed out in **relief**. She didn't want to be in trouble! She and the others agreed that it had been nice of Timmy to speak up, but why had he tried to scare them in the first place?

They all got into their own beds, and Tammy's mum came back and tucked them in.

She kissed Tammy good night first. She whispered quietly that she thought Timmy was trying to show off to impress them because he was so excited to be part of the **Friendship Club!** Hello Kitty, Fifi and Tammy all nodded, and Tammy said she hoped he would stop being silly soon. Her mum grinned – she definitely hoped that too! She'd been having a quiet cup of tea when she'd had to jump out of her chair to come and see what was going on. Tammy offered to make her another cup of tea but her mum said she would be fine. She smiled, and suggested that maybe she should read them a bedtime story instead – what did they think?

The girls loved that idea! So Tammy's mum read them a bedtime story, and when she reached the end she turned the light out. Hello Kitty snuggled down under her duvet. She was feeling **very** tired – it had been a very eventful day, that was for sure! What would tomorrow hold?

5

Timmy in Trouble

When the girls got up in the morning, there wasn't a cloud in the sky. They ran downstairs to where Tammy's dad was listening to the radio. He mentioned it was going to be a very hot day. **Hooray!** That meant they could go swimming!

They had toast and cereal for breakfast and

then put on their swimsuits and beach clothes.

Soon everyone was trooping down

to the beach laden

with beach bags,

towels and cold drinks.

Tammy's dad was

even carrying a

small inflatable boat

with paddles!

The sea was just going out as they reached the beach. They all set out the deckchairs and towels near the bottom of the cliff, and Timmy threw off his clothes and ran off down to the water's edge. He jumped straight in! The girls followed him. They could all swim well, but Tammy's mum warned them not to go too deep! She would keep an eye on them all.

When they reached the sea, the water was

very clear – and also still quite cold. Hello Kitty gasped as she paddled in it.

Timmy was already swimming. He told them it was fine when you were in and he did look like he was having a good time, floating on his back and *diving* under the water.

Hello Kitty took a deep breath and started to paddle out through the waves. Tammy came with her. But where was Fifi?

They looked round and saw that she was still on the beach.

Hmmm... Hello Kitty guessed that she was probably a bit worried about jellyfish again. She called out to Fifi that there weren't any jellyfish here; it was quite safe. But Fifi still wasn't sure. What if some jellyfish came along?

Tammy reassured her they wouldn't, but Fifi thought she would still paddle at the edge, just in case.

Hello Kitty and Tammy had a little swim but it wasn't as much fun without Fifi. But then Tammy had an idea! What about the little boat? They could go out in that and then Fifi wouldn't have to be in the water! Hello Kitty **grinned** at her. It was a super plan!

They ran back to ask if they could use the inflatable boat. Tammy's parents said that it would be fine, but Tammy's dad would need to come and watch them from near the water's edge so he could help if they started drifting out too far. He warned them that they had to be careful to make sure they didn't go out too **deep** and get carried out to sea.

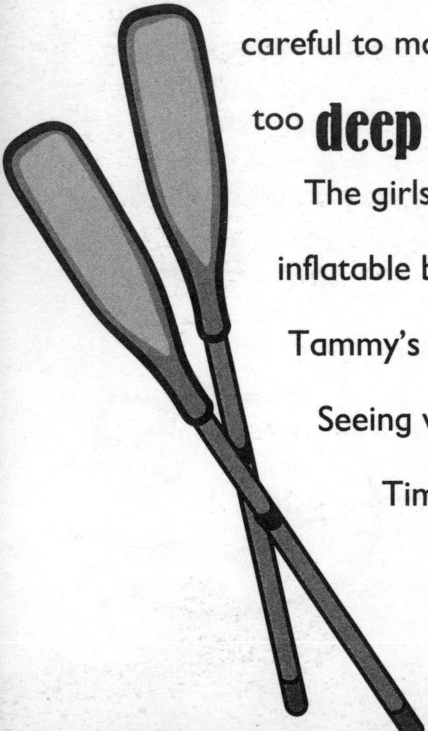

The girls dragged the little inflatable boat to the water while Tammy's dad carried the paddles. Seeing what they were doing, Timmy came over. He wanted to come too!

They all climbed in with the paddles. Fifi **beamed**. This was definitely the best way to go out on to the sea, she declared.

Timmy and Tammy rowed while Fifi and Hello Kitty looked over the sides. The water was really clear and they could see all the way to the bottom!

Just then, Fifi caught her breath as something floated towards them. Was it a jellyfish?

But Tammy fished it out – it was just an old plastic bag! **Yuck!** Fifi was very relieved. But then Timmy said he thought HE could see a jellyfish – a real one.

Hello Kitty could tell he was teasing from the way he was grinning from ear to ear. But Fifi still looked worried.

And then Timmy started rocking the boat from side to side, all the time saying he could still see the jellyfish! Tammy smiled nervously and told him

to stop showing off, as they didn't like it. But he just rocked the boat **even more!** Fifi slipped to one edge and gave a little squeal as she almost fell into the water. Hello Kitty grabbed her just in time.

Tammy and Hello Kitty both shouted at Timmy to stop, and Tammy's dad had seen what was happening too. They weren't very deep, so he came striding out into the water. He spoke sternly to Timmy about scaring Fifi. Timmy said quietly that he was **just** trying to make everyone laugh, but his dad still wasn't very happy with him – and neither were the girls. So Timmy got out of the boat and swam back to the beach with his dad. Fifi was **fine** now that the boat had stopped rocking, so the girls rowed around, enjoying bobbing on the water.

After a while they paddled in to get a drink. Tammy's dad was sitting in his deckchair and the girls decided to go for a walk to collect some shells. It was lovely walking along the soft sand, drinking their ice-cold sodas. But after walking for a while picking up pretty shells, they started wondering where Timmy was.

Suddenly, Hello Kitty heard a shout. She looked up. Timmy was climbing up the steep cliff face just in front of them! He was quite **high**

up. He waved at them and shouted that he bet they wouldn't be brave enough to climb up after him!

The girls were worried. Tammy's parents had told them **not** to climb the cliffs. What if he fell? He might hurt himself! Tammy yelled for him to come down but he just laughed.

Hello Kitty looked round. They had walked quite far from Tammy's parents, and even if they called out they wouldn't hear. What should they do? How could they get Timmy to come down? They all called out to him, and Timmy could see they were worried so he gave a sigh and said he would come back to the beach.

But just as he started to climb down he lost his grip and **slipped!**

The girls all gasped. Luckily Timmy landed on a rocky ledge halfway up the cliff. His face was pale, but he was **OK**. He wasn't sure how he could get down though, he called. He didn't want to slip again! Hello Kitty and the others looked at each other. They had to help him get down. But how could they do that?

6

Rescue!

Hello Kitty saw Tammy and Fifi's scared faces, and decided it was time someone took charge! She took a deep breath, and told Tammy to run and get her mum and dad. Then she shouted to Timmy that she and Fifi would

stay with him until help arrived. It was an easy climb up to the ledge, but Timmy was still too shaken up to get down to the beach on his own.

Tammy hurried off to her mum and dad and Hello Kitty and Fifi climbed up the rocks to Timmy. He was looking very worried, and trying not to cry. But he was **definitely** very happy they were there with him! Hello Kitty gave him a hug and Fifi gave him some sweets she had in her pocket.

Hello Kitty thought about helping him down, but it was a **bit too** risky for them to try. Instead, she and Fifi sat down on either side of him. Hello Kitty asked him why he had climbed up the cliff, and Timmy whispered that he had wanted to show them how brave he was.

Fifi frowned. Why had he wanted to do that?

Timmy looked embarrassed. He said they had made the Friendship Club sound so much fun, he wanted to impress them now that he was in it! Hello Kitty hugged him. He didn't need to impress them – they already thought he was *great!* And they thought he was even better when he wasn't scaring them or showing off, she said with a small smile.

Timmy hung his head. He thought he'd really messed things up. He was worried they wouldn't want him to be part of the Friendship Club any more, he said.

Fifi squeezed his arm. Of course they still wanted him to be a member of the Friendship Club, she declared – well, so long as he stopped pretending that he had seen a jellyfish! Timmy **Smiled**. He guessed he could do that!

Just then, Tammy's parents arrived. Tammy's dad climbed up the cliff to help them all down – Hello Kitty and Fifi first, followed by Timmy.

Once the girls reached the bottom, Tammy's mum gave them a great big hug and thanked them for looking after Timmy and fetching help. Then she reached out to Timmy, who had just been helped down by his dad. **Luckily** he wasn't hurt. He would be OK, but there would be no more climbing up cliffs. Timmy definitely agreed with that!

Timmy's parents walked them back to the picnic. They'd need to think of something else to do for the day now because Timmy was a bit too shaken to play on the beach much. What could they do? **Hmmm...**

Hello Kitty thought she might know! She

glanced at Tammy, and from the look on her face she knew they had the same idea. They just had to persuade Tammy and Timmy's parents to agree...

Luckily, Tammy's parents thought it was the perfect idea! After lunch, they went to where the boats were and Tammy's dad spoke to one of the boat owners. Soon they were all strapped in on one of the boats, wearing orange life

jackets and **whizzing** out across the sea. They *were* going on a boat trip after all!

As the boat sped across the waves, Hello Kitty breathed in the salty spray and felt a warm rush of happiness. She was in a boat with her friends, having the perfect holiday treat.

She even had a new Friendship Rule going round in her head. She couldn't wait to share it with the others…

She hoped they would like it. After all, there was no need for a friend to ever show off because friends like you exactly as you are. Fifi was just saying that she thought beach holidays were the **best** when the boat's owner slowed the boat down, and told them to take a look out over the sea....

Suddenly, a round head with big brown puppy-dog eyes popped up out of the water!

And then another.

And another.

They were seals!

The girls clapped their hands in delight as the seals swum over. They were so beautiful. Hello Kitty **almost** touched one as it swam past, and Tammy gasped as they bobbed up and down near the boat. Fifi giggled and beamed, and took a picture of them with her camera.

Then Tammy's mum got them all together so she could take a photo of the three girls and Timmy in the boat together, with the seals in the water behind them! Hello Kitty grinned at the camera with the others. She felt super-lucky to be on a holiday like this with her friends!

They'd already done lots of exciting things, and there were still two whole days to go!

As the boat left the seals and sped off across the *sparkling* water, Hello Kitty breathed in the salty air. Oh yes, beach holidays really were the best!

HELLO KITTY'S FRIENDSHIP FUN!

Turn over the page for activities and fun things that you can do with your friends – just like Hello Kitty!

Activity 1

Write your own story!

Hello Kitty and her friends love to make up stories – it's one of their favourite things! Follow the instructions and ideas on the following pages to get you started, and then you can make up a story of your very own…

Interesting Ideas!

Every story has to start somewhere. It can be an idea, a word, or even a picture! Think about some of your favourite things, or even somewhere fun you have been – like the beach! Then you can start to think of what the story you want to tell is about, and who will be in it.

Hmmm... What to Do?

The best stories often have a problem that needs to be solved, and all stories need to have something happen in them! Think about what could happen in yours – it can be something that has happened to you, or something you have just made up.

Characters

Who is in your story? Every story needs characters – heroes and bad guys; clever ones and funny ones! Who can be in yours? Maybe even you or your friends…

Where to go today?

Where is your story going to happen? It can be somewhere fun, like on holiday, or somewhere exciting – like a spaceship! It can be anywhere you want, so get thinking…

Titles

When you have written your story, the last thing you need is a title! A good title can tell you what's inside a book… or even just make you want to find out! What will yours be?

Magic and mischief!

Anything can happen in stories. You can have magical powers, or see strange and exciting things – like a unicorn, or a robot! Things can happen that are funny, or exciting, or even a little bit scary. Pick whatever you want, and see how it will fit in.

Once Upon a Time

Stories can happen whenever you want too. It could be today, or in the olden days, or even in 100 years time! What time will work for your story – it might be better in the future if you're going to meet a robot!

Get started!

Getting started can be the hardest thing about writing a story! If you're having trouble starting, here are some ideas for first lines that might help:

It was a hot day when Hello Kitty looked out over the beach. She could see something in the distance… but what was it?

Phew! Dear Daniel had been taking photos of animals all day, and was looking forward to a rest. But suddenly…

When Fifi was a little girl, she had always wanted a pet. But she had never imagined she would have a magical one!

Tammy ran through the spaceship as fast as she could. Her robot friend Timmy was gliding along with her, and as she looked at him he said…

Activity 2

Hello Kitty's Summer Punch

Phew... it can be hot on the beach! Hello Kitty and her friends know how important it is to keep cool, and what better way to do it than with an icy cold drink? This summer punch recipe is super-yummy and will make lots of punch for you and your friends!

You will need:

I litre of Lemonade

I litre of Ginger Ale

500ml of Pineapple Juice

500ml of Orange Juice

250ml Blackcurrant Squash

Strawberries

Mint leaves

To make the punch:

1. Mix together the pineapple juice, orange juice and blackcurrant squash in a big bowl or jug.
2. Wash and chop up the mint leaves and strawberries, and stir them in.
3. Chill the mixture in the fridge for at least an hour.
4. Just before you serve, mix the lemonade and ginger ale in, so they stay fizzy. But stir slowly so it doesn't fizz over!
5. Serve over a glass full of ice, and enjoy!

Decorate each glass of punch with an extra strawberry and a sprig of mint, or even some rainbow sprinkles. Delicious!

Turn the page for a sneak peek at

HELLO KITTY and friends'

next adventure...

The Treasure Hunt

Hello Kitty put the paper into a neat pile on the shelves of the school art cupboard. She'd already sorted the paintbrushes into different pots and sharpened the pencils, and put them all away.

Her teacher Miss Davey came in, and took a look around. A big smile spread over her face as she exclaimed at what a great job Hello Kitty had done! The cupboard had never been so tidy. Miss

Davey thanked her for all her hard work, and for volunteering to clear it out. It had taken Hello Kitty most of her lunch break.

Hello Kitty had been very happy to help! She asked if Miss Davey needed her to finish sorting the paints out by colour, but Miss Davey told her that they could leave that for another day. Hello Kitty nodded happily and skipped off to find her friends. She loved helping people!

Her friends Tammy and Fifi were sitting at a table in their empty classroom, heads bent over pieces of paper. It was strange not seeing Dear Daniel with them. Dear Daniel was Hello Kitty's other really good friend but he was away travelling with his dad, and was missing the first few days of the school term – he had gotten permission for it earlier in the year. Hello Kitty was organising a big welcome home party for him in three days time. She still needed to get some decorations and food and sort out the games, and she made a list in her head as she went over to where Fifi and Tammy were sitting. Suddenly, one of her special, super, Hello Kitty ideas popped into her head. Instead of games, what about having a treasure hunt?

Hello Kitty squealed excitedly, and Fifi and Tammy looked up as she quickly started to tell them her idea for Dear Daniel's welcome home party.

Fifi smiled distractedly, and rubbed something out on her paper.

Tammy nodded and agreed that it was a great idea, but she only looked up for a moment.

Hello Kitty blinked. She had thought her friends would be much more excited! Fifi pushed her paper away, and looked up at Hello Kitty again. She sighed, and explained to Hello Kitty that she was sorry she was so distracted. She was trying to design an ice-skating costume for her new routine, as she hadn't been able to find anything that was just right. She had thought it would be easy, but designing an outfit was harder than she thought!

Tammy piped up that she was trying to make up a story for the school magazine. She had the beginning done, but couldn't decide what should happen next, and it had to be handed in on Friday!

But they both thought Hello Kitty's idea of a welcome home treasure hunt did sound good. Hello Kitty smiled and thanked them, before declaring that they didn't need to worry about that for now – it sounded like they needed her help!

Fifi and Tammy both brightened up at this. Hello Kitty was so good at designing clothes, so Fifi knew she'd be a great help with her costume!

And Tammy was just as excited that she would be able to tell her what she'd written in her story so far, and have her help come up with what would happen next. Hello Kitty grinned. There was nothing she liked better than helping her friends…

Find out what happens next in…

Win Hello Kitty Goodies and prizes!

Collect the secret passwords in the first six Hello Kitty and Friends books, and go to **www.harpercollins.co.uk/HelloKittyandFriends** to download your exclusive Hello Kitty activities, games and fun!

Collect all six secret passwords to win super-special goodies!*

Coming soon:

*...e stocks last. One password redeemable per book purchase, prizes limited to three per household.